Almost Summer

Almost Summer 1

Translated by Helge Dascher and Robin Lang
Visual adaptation by the author and Vincent Giard
Copy-edited by Rupert Bottenberg

ISBN 978-2-924049-39-6

www.powpowpress.com
Montreal, Canada

First paperback edition: February 2017. Printed in Canada by Imprimerie Gauvin.

Conseil des arts   Canada Council
du Canada   for the Arts

Nous remercions le Conseil des arts du Canada de son soutien. L'an dernier, le Conseil a investi 153 millions de dollars pour mettre de l'art dans la vie des Canadiennes et des Canadiens de tout le pays.

We acknowledge the support of the Canada Council for the Arts, which last year invested $153 million to bring the arts to Canadians throughout the country.

Nous reconnaissons l'aide financière du gouvernement du Québec par l'entremise de la Société de développement des entreprises culturelles (SODEC) pour nos activités d'édition.

Sophie Bédard

Almost Summer

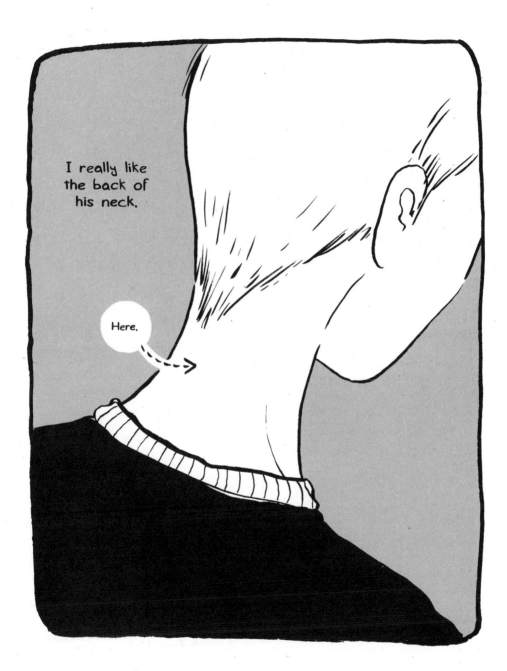

Who cares
what Mimi says.

I don't really mind that I'm
the least athletic person at
school (or in the world).

I just hate having *him*
see me fail so bad.

What's it
going to
be?

20 cm?

Ughh.

One thing I hate
about my school

is that the teachers
always make us sit in
alphabetical order at the
start of the school year.

And so I'm always
behind him.

Always
always
always.

It's not just that my
family name comes
right after his,

but he's been in the
my home room for
the past four years.

Ha. Ha. Ha.

Meanwhile...

94

123

S.BÉDARD

To be continued...

Also by Pow Pow Press

Graphic novels

For as Long as It Rains, Zviane, 2015
Mile End, Michel Hellman, 2015
Vile and Miserable, Samuel Cantin, 2015
Vampire Cousins, Cathon and Alexandre Fontaine Rousseau, 2015
Going Under, Zviane, 2016
Earthbound, Blonk, 2016
Art Wars, Francis Desharnais, 2016
Nunavik, Michel Hellman, 2017
Gary, King of the Pickup Artists, Alexandre Simard and Luc Bossé, 2017

Sketchbooks

Croquis de Québec, Guy Delisle, 2013
Dessins, Pascal Girard, 2014

www.powpowpress.com